PUFFIN BOOKS

Galactic Snapshots

Kenneth Oppel wrote his first children's book when he was a-fifteen-year-old high school student in Victoria, British Columbia. Since then he has studied cinema and English literature at the University of Toronto, and written over a dozen books for both children and young adults, as well as several screenplays. He lives in Canada with his wife, Philippa.

KENNETH OPPEL

Galactic Snapshots

Illustrated by Guy Parker-Rees

PUFFIN BOOKS

For Philippa

PUFFIN BOOKS

Published by the Penguin Group
Penguin Books Ltd, 27 Wrights Lane, London W8 5TZ, England
Penguin Books USA Inc., 375 Hudson Street, New York, New York 10014, USA
Penguin Books Australia Ltd, Ringwood, Victoria, Australia
Penguin Books Canada Ltd, 10 Alcorn Avenue, Toronto, Ontario, Canada M4V 3B2
Penguin Books (NZ) Ltd, 182–190 Wairau Road, Auckland 10, New Zealand

Penguin Books Ltd, Registered Offices: Harmondsworth, Middlesex, England

Galactic Snapshots
First published by Hamish Hamilton 1993
Cosmic Snapshots
First published by Hamish Hamilton 1993
This omnibus edition published in Puffin Books 1996
10 9 8 7 6 5 4 3 2 1

Text copyright © Kenneth Oppel, 1993
Illustrations copyright © Guy Parker-Rees, 1993
All rights reserved

The moral right of the author has been asserted

Filmset in Baskerville

Made and printed in England by Clays Ltd, St Ives plc

Contents

Chapter One

My own camera! Finally!

I was so excited I was charging around the house, taking pictures of everything in sight. My toothbrush! A piece of toast! A scab that had just dropped off my knee into the carpet! It was fantastic.

"Mum, do something funny!"

Through my viewfinder, I saw her growl and shake her fist at me.

I don't think she was joking, but it made a good picture anyway.

Click!

"Thanks, Mum!"

"Why did you give him your old camera?" she asked my father with a sigh. "It's bad enough having one photographer in the family."

"It's a perfect opportunity for him to learn," Dad told her. "I had my first camera when I was about Ian's age."

My dad's a professional photographer. He's even won prizes for his pictures. Some of them hang framed in our sitting room. For the longest time, I'd wanted a camera of my own.

"Come here, Fuzz," I said, calling our cat over.

"Stop tormenting that poor animal," said Mum. "You've taken enough pictures of her already!"

"But I've only got one left!" I protested.

"I think," said my mother firmly, "that you need some practice at outdoor photography!"

The sky was lead grey and there was electricity in the air. It felt like a storm coming.

I walked down the lane to the field behind our house. A fat drop of rain splashed my arm, and I heard a distant drumroll of thunder. I was about to turn back when a fork of lightning suddenly stabbed across the sky.

"Wow!" I gasped. "Now *that* would make a great picture!"

I lifted the camera to my face, hoping for more fireworks.

Within seconds the sky was split in half by a jagged stroke of blue lightning.

Click!

It all happened so fast, I was worried I might have missed it.

I'd never seen blue lightning before!

Chapter Two

The darkroom was my favourite
place in the world. I'd practically
grown up in the darkroom, watching
my dad develop his films and make
prints.

But this time it was my own film
we were developing!

I watched expectantly as the
lightning bolt picture came into view.
I made out some trees, a bit of the

sky. But down the whole right-hand side of the picture, where the lightning bolt should have been, was a long dark smudge.

"Why did that happen?" I asked.

"It may have been too bright for the camera," said Dad.

"Oh."

"Don't worry," said Dad, clapping me on the shoulder. "It's not your fault. It was a very difficult shot. Be patient. Here's another roll of film for you to practise with."

"Thanks," I said. "Can I use the darkroom when you're away?"

"No. Only when I'm here, Ian,

you know the rules. We can develop it when I get back in a few days from my assignment, OK?"

"OK," I said, already thinking of new snapshots I could take.

The next day, I brought my camera to school to show Peter and Malcolm. While they were looking at it, I was watching Sean Harlowe from the corner of my eye, kind of hoping he'd notice, too.

But as usual he was too busy.

Sean traded things. Every day at school, he was wheeling and dealing. He was a genius at it. The inside of his desk was like a treasure chest. Sean always boasted that he could turn a busted pencil into a new bike before the end of the week. I believed him.

We used to be best friends until, one day, he borrowed my gym shoes, and I never saw them again – well, I saw them on someone else's feet, but that wasn't much good to me! I guess Sean traded them for something he just couldn't resist. I didn't talk to him much after that.

"Hey, where'd you get that?" Sean said suddenly, looking at my camera.

"My dad gave it to me."

A glint came into his eyes.

"I'll trade you for it."

I'd been waiting for that.

"Sorry," I said with a big smile.

Before I could stop him, he'd snatched the pile of photos off my

8

desk and was waving them in the air.

"Hey, everyone! Look at all Ian's snapshots! Ooh, I like this nice big smudge here!" he said, pointing at my lightning bolt snapshot. "Very artistic!"

"Give them back!" I said angrily, grabbing back the pictures.

I sat glaring at the smudged photo. It was terrible. Then I frowned. At the bottom right-hand corner of the snapshot was an odd shadow. It almost looked like a small car, one of those tiny ones with only three wheels – maybe even smaller.

Funny, I hadn't noticed it yesterday when I took the picture.

After school, I'd go back to have a look.

In the field, I used the photograph like a map. But when I got to the right spot, all I saw was a small patch of scorched grass.

"This must be where the blue bolt of lightning hit," I said to myself.

I reached for my camera. It might make a good photograph.

Click!

I took a few steps closer to get one more shot –

"Ow!" I cried, as pain shot up my knee.

I staggered back in amazement.

I'd just banged my knee on thin air!

It made no sense! There had to be something there! I grabbed a rock and was about to toss it –

When I crashed down hard on my bum, and the camera flew right out of my hands, up into the air. It seemed to be taking an awfully long time coming back down. Dazed, I watched as it just hung there,

jiggling around a bit. Then, all by itself, it started shooting off pictures like crazy.

Click!

Click-click-click!

Then it dropped back into my lap.

For a few seconds, all I could do was stare at it.

Then I got up and ran.

All the film in my camera had been shot off.

12

I sat on my bed, still out of breath. Something very strange had happened out there in the field. Something invisible . . .

I glanced quickly at the camera.

Something that could only be seen in photographs!

I didn't know for sure, but maybe if I developed the film, I'd have a better idea of what happened out there!

Dad wouldn't be back for another two days. I couldn't wait till then! This was important. I knew where he kept the keys. I knew how to mix all the chemicals and work the equipment – I'd watched Dad enough times to do it in my sleep! And afterwards I'd put everything away so carefully he'd never notice.

But when would I do it? There wasn't enough time now. Mum would be home from work soon.

It would have to be in the dead of night!

I carefully poured the chemicals into the trays.

I was shivering, partly with the cold, partly with excitement. I tightened my jaw to stop my teeth chattering. It was two o'clock in the morning.

I gently swished the paper around in the developing tray. This was supposed to be the snapshot of the scorched grass. But, as the picture swam into view, there was no grass in sight.

Instead, it was that same strange
shape I'd seen before, only much
closer up. It didn't look like a car
any more.

I'd smashed my knee against a
spaceship!

With trembling hands, I started on
all the snapshots the camera had
taken by itself. One after the other,
they came out as crooked pictures of

the cloudy sky, with maybe a few
blurry treetops jutting in from the
corners.

Then I came to the last one.

I started shivering so hard I nearly
fell over.

I saw sky, some clouds, a couple of
trees.

But in the lower corner was a
head.

The only way I knew it was a
head, was because of the eyes.

All four of them.

Chapter Three

School was dragging on for ever, and it was only first class.

I went over my plan for the hundredth time.

I needed more photographs.

The ones I had weren't good enough. No one would believe them. Especially not the one of the alien. It was too blurry, and you could only see the head. I needed the whole

alien, and more of the spaceship.
After school I'd go back to the field.

And then I'd have the only set of
galactic snapshots in the world!

Dad would be proud of me.

Sean would eat his words.

I'd be famous.

But first, school had to get out!

As I neared the field, I decided to
sneak around through the trees, just
in case the alien was watching for
me. Suddenly I felt nervous.

What if this alien was dangerous?

What if he ate people!

I peered through some branches near the scorched patch of grass. I raised the camera to my eye.

"How now, thou sneaking knave!"

The voice was high and fluty and seemed to echo slightly. I'd never heard anything like it! It could only be the voice of something from another planet! A space alien speaking English! And what strange English it was!

Slowly I turned round.

Of course, there was nothing to see.

"Now, sir," came the invisible voice, this time at my right, "why do you skulk about in this lowly fashion?"

"I . . . I wanted to take some

pictures of you," I stammered.

"Ah! So that is the purpose of that device. How treacherous!"

"I haven't taken any yet," I said weakly.

"Nor shall you!" the alien shrilled.

"Are you going to eat me?" I squeaked.

"Most definitely not!" said the alien indignantly. "We have been advised not to dine on the local animals."

"Animals?" I said, blinking.

"You, sir," said the alien.

This was a little much.

"I'm not an animal," I said, "I'm a human being."

"Psshaw!" said the alien disdainfully. "You, sir, are most primitive."

20

"At least I don't talk like I'm four hundred years old!"

"It is taught thusly at my school," said the alien snootily, and then added, "We have all studied *The Complete Works of William Shakespeare*."

"Have you come here to study us, then?"

"No. We have small interest in you."

"Oh," I said, a little put out. This alien didn't have a very high opinion of us. "So why did you come?"

"A game," said the alien. "In this game, everyone hides, except for one person, whose task it is to find the others."

"Hide-and-seek!" I exclaimed.

21

"You're playing hide-and-seek on our planet!"

"Your galaxy," the alien corrected me.

The idea made me a little dizzy. But I was starting to feel more relaxed now. Maybe this space alien wasn't so different from me. He played hide-and-seek, he went to school. Heck, he was even forced to read Shakespeare!

I was about to ask the alien how old he was, when suddenly he flickered into view.

It was only a split second, but long enough for me to see that strange head of his, and the rest of his body. I think he had more arms, or maybe more legs than me, but the most unusual thing was his colour.

He was bright orange!

Then he disappeared again.

"Zounds!" the alien exclaimed.
"My invisibility engine falters! It
hides my humble space craft,
and myself, from the likes of
you."

"You show up in pictures
though," I told him.

"I feared as much," said the alien
miserably.

"Can't I just take a couple of
snapshots?"

"These pictures, why do you
desire them so?"

"Well . . . "

"You would show them to others,
would you not? You hope to use

them for your own fame and fortune!"

The way he said it made me feel ashamed.

I nodded.

"Listen well, then," said the alien. "Long ago, before the invisibility engines, an ancestor of mine crashed on this planet. He was captured, and people thought he was a monster! A demon! He was put in prison, and there he died."

"But you can always zoom off in your spaceship, if things get rough, can't you?"

The alien was silent for a moment.

"Nay," he said quietly. "My spacecraft was struck by a bolt of lightning! I have run aground!

I am unable to leave."

"Oh," I said.

Once again the alien flashed before me.

"I am in most grievous danger," he said. "I need time to repair my craft. 'Ere long I will run out of energy, and then the invisibility engine will die. I will be seen by all!"

I took a deep breath.

"Can I do anything?"

"Yes," said the alien. "Take no pictures. Tell no one. Promise me that."

"All right," I said reluctantly. "I promise."

Chapter Four

All next day in school, I was thinking about William.

Of course, William wasn't his real name. I didn't know his real name. Even if I did, I probably wouldn't have been able to pronounce it! But since he'd learned English from Shakespeare, I thought William was a pretty good choice.

I'd told him I'd come again after

school, to see if I could help with anything. But the day was crawling by.

In Maths class, Sean gave me a very sly look.

"Hey, is this a picture of you, Ian?" he whispered.

I felt ice go through my veins. When I turned around to look, I nearly cried out. He must have slipped it out of my satchel. It was my one and only picture of William!

"Good shot of you," smirked Sean.

"Um, yeah, thanks," I said, deciding to play along with it. "It's a pretty neat mask, isn't it?"

He gave me a funny look.

"You're up to something, Ian."

I snatched back the picture and

stuffed it into my satchel. My hand
was shaking.

William kept flickering on and off
like a faulty orange light bulb.
   "My energy is fast disappearing,"
he said miserably.
   "Maybe you can hide at my
house," I suggested.
   "You are kind, but not only does

the invisibility engine hide us, it also protects us from your sun. If I tarry too long in its glare, I will surely perish!"

'Well, how are the repairs coming?" I asked worriedly. "Any luck?"

"The damage, I fear, is irreparable."

I sighed and looked over at his spaceship. We'd dragged it into the trees and covered it with leaves. But I could still see it flickering away, underneath.

"Look, maybe a mechanic could –"

"Hah!" interrupted William. "I do strongly doubt that any craftsman on this globe could fix such a craft as mine!"

I was about to protest, when I heard something from the trees.

I whirled around.

Sean was standing at the edge of the clearing.

"Gotcha!" he said, and started to run.

"Wait! Sean, come back!" I shouted.

I chased after him across the field, launched myself at his heels and we both went tumbling to the grass.

"I knew you were up to something!" Sean panted as we wrestled. "I saw you yesterday, like you were talking to nobody! And then that picture in class! You've got yourself an alien!"

"You can't tell anyone!"

"Why not?"

"It's a secret!"

"It's a gold mine! Think of all the pictures you could take, Ian! That's what you want, isn't it?"

I let go of him. He was right. I was just as bad as he was. It made me feel sick.

"If he stays here much longer," I said, "he might die."

"Why?" Sean asked, sitting up.

"The sun. It's too bright for him or something."

"Oh."

"Do you want to meet him?" I asked.

Sean nodded eagerly.

"First promise me you won't tell."

"Deal," he said.

"So, you've got a busted spaceship," said Sean awkwardly.

He didn't know what to say. He was so excited, he just stood there, hands in pockets, nodding mindlessly.

"Various parts need replacing," the alien replied.

When William said that, an idea dropped into my head.

"Sean can get you spare parts," I blurted out.

"For an alien space ship?" Sean exclaimed. "Are you crazy?"

"You always said you could get anything by trading," I reminded him.

"Yeah, but – "

"Can't do it?" I said, raising

my eyebrows.

I saw the glint come back into his eyes.

"I'll consider it a personal challenge."

I'd never seen Sean work so hard.

He bargained. He traded. He called in favours. He was brilliant.

The next day at recess we went to the mechanic's and showed him the diagram William had drawn for us.

"Can you make us this part?" Sean asked.

"I don't know," the mechanic replied. "It looks . . . unusual."

"Listen, Bob," said Sean firmly, "who fixed you up with that heater last winter? You owe me a favour."

"All right, all right," said Bob,

firing up his gas torch.

At lunch we went to the electronics shop and Sean strutted in as if he owned the place. He did a little talking, and before I knew it, a sales clerk was running around, picking out resistors and capacitors and who knows what else.

It was the same thing at the computer repair shop. I just stood back and watched as Sean bargained for more alien spaceship spare parts. It was truly inspirational.

"You deserve a medal," I said to Sean outside.

After school we picked everything up, packed it carefully into a box and ran all out for the field.

We'd almost reached the field when a little girl roared past us, her face white as milk, her eyes bulging like marbles.

"Monster!" she screamed.

"There's an orange monster in the field!"

Sean and I sped up. When we reached the clearing, William was peering out from the hatch in his spacecraft. Neither were flickering any more. They were both completely visible, and William was very, very orange. It almost hurt to look at him.

"Methinks I've been found out!" he said.

"Yep," I said.

"We've got the parts," said Sean, opening the box.

"Most excellent," said William, taking a look. "Perchance I was overly hasty in calling you primitive. Now then . . ."

He ducked down into his spaceship.

"Hmmm, uhhh, ohhhh," he said from inside.

"How's it going?" I asked impatiently.

"The parts are crude indeed," said William, "but thus far, they do seem to be working."

In the distance, I heard the whine of a police siren.

"You'd better hurry up!" I hissed.

"Alas! It's to no avail!" exclaimed William suddenly. He stuck his head through the hatch. "There is one piece that simply refuses to fit!"

I peeked out through the trees. In the distance, I could see two policemen making their way across the field, with big dogs on leads.

"Look, we've got to hide you!" I whispered. "Get inside and we'll dump more leaves on top!"

"Be still!" said William suddenly. "Listen!"

"What?" I said impatiently.

"I have been caught!" he exclaimed.

"Not yet, you great twit!" I snapped. "But you will be if you don't shut up!"

"You mistake me, sir! Look!"

He pointed with an orange finger.

The sky suddenly burst apart and a big bolt of blue lightning scorched through the air towards us. Leaves and grit and hot air blew into my face so I could hardly see. It felt

38

like the end of the world!

And then I suddenly remembered.

The game of hide-and-seek!

The invisible spaceship must have landed in the clearing, because another orange alien suddenly appeared at William's side.

"Hrrggrretchyyvoooovvk!" William said, or something like that.

"Jbkekkkqqqquikkk!" the other alien replied, or something like that.

Sean and I looked at each other and shrugged.

"We must make haste!" said William, turning to face me.

His friend seemed to be hooking up some sort of tow-line between their two ships.

"Do you think you might come

back sometime?" I asked.

"You have my solemn vow," he promised. "And perhaps then you may take my picture!"

"How do you feel about TV appearances?" Sean asked, then added, "Only joking."

"Good-bye, William," I said.

I'd never called him that, but he seemed to understand, because he smiled and gave a little bow.

"I am most honoured by the name," he said. "And now, we're away! My thanks to you both!"

William and his friend jumped inside their ships.

The hatches clanged shut.

Then they shot straight up into the sky in another bolt of blue lightning.

When I got home, I found Dad in the sitting room, reading the newspaper. He gave me a big hug.

"So, tell me what you've been up to. Did you get any interesting snapshots?"

"Oh, only one of a space alien," I said carelessly, "but it didn't turn out very well."

"Too bad," said my father with a chuckle. "Well, maybe you'll get another chance one day, you never know."

"You never know," I said, smiling out at the evening sky.

Cosmic Snapshots

For Philippa

Chapter One

"First prize," said Mr Bruckman from the front of the classroom, "will be awarded to the most exciting and original snapshot. Now, who's interested in entering? Let's have a show of hands."

A photo contest! Both my hands shot up into the air.

My dad's a professional photographer, and ever since he gave me one of his old cameras, I've been taking pictures of everything in sight!

My mum thinks I've gone around the bend. So do our neighbours. So does our cat, who runs whenever she sees me with my camera. But I can tell my dad's secretly pleased. Like father, like son. I want to be a famous photographer just like him. Maybe this contest would give me the chance to prove myself!

I glanced over at Sean Harlowe, hoping he wasn't interested in the contest, too.

As usual, he was busy trading things at the back of the classroom. I suppose you could call Sean a genius. He could get anything he wanted by trading. He's always boasting he

could turn a box of paperclips into a
colour television by the end of the
week. I believe him.

Sometimes, Sean and I are best
friends, and sometimes we're worst
enemies. We're usually best friends
until I see someone colouring with
my felt-tipped pens, or eating my
lunch, or reading the comic book I
had in my desk a few hours ago – and

I know Sean's traded them without telling me.

You have to keep your eye on him.

Right now, I could tell he was working on something pretty big.

By the first bell he had Chris Thornton's new pack of pencil crayons.

By the second bell he had Gina Larowski's toy helicopter.

By the third bell he had a portable radio.

It was just as well he was all tied up. I knew he didn't have a camera of his own, but I didn't want him interfering with my chances of winning first prize.

When the last bell finally sounded,

I leaped from my seat, dumped my books in my locker, and raced down the hall. I wanted to get started right away.

Sean was waiting for me at the main doors, smiling.

"Don't you want to know what I've been doing all day?" he said.

"No," I told him, "I'd rather not."

"Take a look."

My eyes widened. A camera.

Chapter Two

Boring.

I'd spent most of Saturday taking snapshots of flowers, and trees, and boats on the river, but none of it was exciting or original. I sat down dejectedly on a stump.

And now I was worried about Sean. He had a camera, too. What if he took the winning snapshot?

"Ian," said a voice behind me.

I turned with a start, but there was no one there.

"Well met, Ian!" came the voice again. "It is I – "

"Sean, get lost!" I said grumpily. He must have been hiding in the bushes.

"How now, my earthly friend?" said the invisible voice, right in front of me this time.

I blinked in surprise, and my whole body tingled.

"William!' I exclaimed.

He flashed before me, a bright orange space alien with four eyes and more arms and legs than I could keep straight. I met him a few months ago when his spaceship got struck by lightning, and crashed in

the field behind our house. He had a
machine that made him and his ship
invisible, but they both showed up
on film, and that's how I found out
about him.

"You came back!" I said.

"I gave you my most solemn vow,
did I not?" said William.

I nodded, glad that I'd kept my
promise, too. I hadn't told anyone
about William, not even my dad.

"Why dost thou sit here so broodingly?" he inquired.

I couldn't help smiling at the way he talked. Everyone at his school learned English from the *Complete Works of William Shakespeare*. That's why I called him William.

"I'm trying to take snapshots for a contest at school," I told him. "They're supposed to be exciting and original. But everything here just looks boring to me. I don't suppose you'd let me take *your* picture this time, would you?"

"Methinks," William replied, "you will find more enthralling things in the heavens above."

He looked at me with a twinkle in his eyes – all four of them.

"You're going to take me into outer space!" I exclaimed.

"In recompense for your past kindness to me. Perchance it might amuse thee?"

"Are you kidding? A tour of the galaxy!"

"Nay, the cosmos!"

"What's the difference?"

"The cosmos is somewhat larger."

"Fantastic!" I said, and then frowned. "Can you have me home in time for dinner?"

"With ease," said William. "Come. My ship is yonder."

Blast off!

As the spaceship rocketed into the sky, I watched the field and the

54

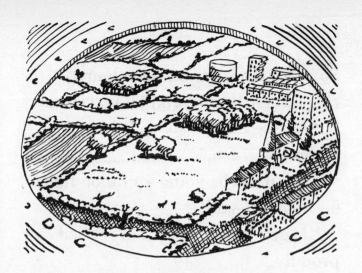

neighbourhood and the town
plummet beneath us. Soon, the Earth
was a blue and green ball
surrounded by blackness, and getting
smaller by the second.

I suddenly felt homesick.

"Do not fret," said William kindly.
"Our journey is but brief."

We were streaking past all the
planets I'd learned about in science
class. Mars, the red planet, then

Saturn with its rainbow-coloured rings, then Jupiter and all its moons! I think we hung a sharp left just before Neptune.

"We must be going a million miles an hour!" I said.

"Much faster," William replied proudly.

"What kind of things will I see?"

"Many wondrous sights. But there is one in particular, which promises to be extraordinary."

"What's that?"

"A planet is going to explode."

"A whole planet?" I spluttered.

"It is but small. Does this disappoint thee?" he asked with concern.

"Well, no. It's just that – well, are

there people on this planet."

William laughed.

"Oh no, nothing liveth there. It is the vilest of planets. No tears will be shed over its demise. It has hidden from view a goodly, pretty solar system for many an age now."

An exploding planet! If this didn't win me the photo contest, nothing would.

There was a clanking sound behind us and we both turned around in surprise. Frowning, William lifted up a hatch in the floor.

"Hi, everybody!"

It was Sean. And he'd brought his camera, too!

Chapter Three

"Sean, you sneak!" I exclaimed.
"You've been following me around!"

"Just seeing what the genius
photographer was doing," he replied
with a devious grin. "Pretty boring
stuff, if you don't mind me saying so,
Ian. All those flowers and – "

"So you thought you'd just stow
away on William's spaceship!"

"You think I was going to pass up

a tour of the cosmos? No way!
Besides, William's my friend, too. I
helped fix his spaceship, remember?"

"Hmm," I grumbled.

"Indeed, I remember it well," said
William with a laugh. "And both of
you are most welcome on this
voyage."

"Great!" said Sean. "I'm going to
win first prize in the photo contest!"

"Oh no you're not," I said angrily.
"*I'm* going to win first prize!"

"Truly, there are wonders enough
in the cosmos for you both!" said
William.

"Well, as long as I get the best
ones," Sean said.

"You should be thrown
overboard," I muttered.

"Methinks the two of you should look out of the windows now," said William.

I turned and gasped.

A blazing green sun blinked on and off like a giant traffic light. And I'd never seen such strange planets! Some were round, but most were diamond-shaped, or perfectly square! In the distance were glittering stars of every possible colour. Floating off the shore of one planet was a vast space city, with thousands of glass domes and bridges. Spaceships glided silently all around us, dipping down or bobbing up from other planets.

I started taking pictures like crazy. Click! Click-click-click!

Luckily for me, Sean seemed more
interested in William's spaceship
than what was outside. I was glued
to the window as we weaved our way
through a meteor field, where huge
worker robots drilled into the rocks.
But Sean was busy poking around,

looking intently at all the buttons and switches and humming machinery.

"How much would you say a spaceship like this costs?" he asked William.

'A vast sum by your earthly terms," replied William with a smile.

"I don't suppose you'd be interested in a trade," said Sean.

"Sadly, no."

"Can I press this button?"

"I think not."

"Why?"

"We would plunge hopelessly through the heavens!"

"What about this one?"

"Prithee, no! We would burst into countless specks of light!"

"Oh," Sean said. 'Well, how about this little switch over here?"

"My good sir!" cried William. "Is my English so paltry that you understand me not? Let me speak more plainly. Lay hands on nothing in this craft!"

Sean skulked back to the window.

"Touchy, isn't he?" he whispered to me. "I mean, how different can it be from a car? I bet I could drive this thing."

He looked out the window with a bored expression.

"I guess I should take some pictures, huh?"

Up ahead I noticed a round patch of perfect blackness, no stars, no planets, nothing. To our right was a

huge billboard, with swirling red and blue lights, and big writing in a language I couldn't understand.

"What does that sign say?" I asked William.

"It doth say: 'Danger. Black Hole Ahead.'"

"A black hole!"

I'd heard about black holes in science class. They were supposed to be like big whirlpools that sucked in absolutely everything, including light!

"Why are we headed straight for it?" I asked nervously.

"We must make haste. This path is shorter."

"You mean into the black hole?" Sean asked.

"You have it precisely, my earthly friend."

"But isn't that dangerous?" I wanted to know.

"Many times have I done this," said William proudly, "and not once have I been caught by the galactic sheriff!"

He winked one of his four eyes at us. "But telleth not thy parents."

"Oh, great!" said Sean. "Ian, you didn't tell me we were travelling with a hot-rodder!"

We were speeding up now, and the spaceship was beginning to shudder.

"If I remember rightly," William said excitedly, "we should arrive at the farthest side of the galaxy."

"Should?" I said meekly.

"It hath never failed me yet."

"We're goners!" cried Sean.

We were swirling around and around the black hole, like water twirling down some giant drain,

faster and faster. There was nothing but pure blackness beyond the windows.

Then suddenly we didn't seem to be moving at all. Everything was frozen like a photograph. I couldn't even blink my eyes! I wasn't breathing! But I didn't seem to need any air. Time had stopped altogether!

Then, just as suddenly, stars were blazing through the windows, I was breathing again, and everything was back to normal.

"Like magic, is it not?" said William.

He swung the spaceship round and pointed through the window.

"We arriveth."

Chapter Four

I could see why no one liked the planet. It was black and pimply, with a big, jagged crack running down one side. Swirls of sickly green smoke drifted across it.

"It will not be long now," said William.

"Can't we go any closer?" Sean asked impatiently.

"I hardly think thou shalt want to

68

be closer once it explodes," William told him.

All around the planet I could see the twinkling lights of lots of other spaceships. It was definitely a big event, like some intergalactic fireworks display. I imagined all these alien families with picnic lunches, sprawled in garden chairs in front of their spaceship windows, doing a little space tanning.

I got my camera ready.

And then the planet exploded.

There was no sound, no big boom, just eerie silence as the planet crumpled in on itself, then ballooned back to its normal size and burst apart, spewing out fire and light and lava.

It was so bright I had to close my eyes. When I opened them, all that was left of the planet were millions of tiny meteoroids, glittering like fireflies, whizzing through space all around us.

"Wow!" Sean said.

My knees felt trembly. I just hoped my snapshots turned out.

In the distance now, I could see a ring of robin egg blue planets circling a golden sun.

Beside me, William sighed.

"Methinks it is the most beautiful sight in the cosmos."

"Well, it's nice," I said, "but not as beautiful as Earth."

"Pah!" said William. "The Earth is a goodly little globe, but it pales beside the likes of this!"

"It's the best planet in the world!" I said indignantly.

"Nonsense! You yourself hath told me how boring it is!"

"Well, I was just in a bad mood," I mumbled.

There was a sudden crackle of electricity, and all the lights in the spaceship blinked out.

I felt dizzy. My whole body was floating off the floor!

"We have lost gravity!" cried William.

"One button!" came Sean's voice. "One stupid button was all I touched!"

"Sean, you idiot!" I shouted. "You've busted the spaceship!"

I was doing the front crawl in mid-air, but it wasn't getting me very far.

William pushed off from the wall and glided over to the controls.

"The main battery functioneth not," he said.

"Well, this is just great!" said Sean, who was hanging upside-down, with his head bumping against the floor. "This is not what I came for, Ian!"

Through the window, I could see the other spaceships disappearing one by one, heading home.

"Won't they come and help us?" I asked.

"We have no way of signalling to them," William replied grimly.

I don't think I'd ever felt so lonely.

My camera floated past me. The photo contest seemed like the most unimportant thing in the world right now. Here we were, trapped in outer space, all because Sean and I wanted to win a stupid contest. But all at once an idea came to me.

I pushed off and drifted after the camera, snatching it out of the air. Then I floated back to one of the windows.

"Not a good time for sight-seeing, Ian," Sean said.

"Put a cork in it."

I fiddled with the camera, held it up to the window, and took a picture.

Flash!

The camera sent a burst of light into outer space.

"Most excellent!" said William. "A signal flare!"

I flashed the camera again and
again.

"Someone's bound to notice!" I
said.

After a few minutes, I saw the
lights from another spaceship
heading towards us.

"Ingenious!" said William.

"Not bad!" said Sean with an
upside-down smile.

We'd make it home after all.

Chapter Five

"Graaak!" said the first alien
mechanic.

"Kraaalk!" said the second.

"Fraaaklak!" said the third.

"Yes, I see," said William. He
turned to me and Sean. "I'm afraid
we find ourselves in yet another
dilemma. I don't have enough to pay
these good gentlemen."

The three alien mechanics looked

at us impatiently. They were the only ones standing upright, because they had special boots with suction cups on the bottom. They came from a different planet than William, and they didn't look very friendly.

I rummaged through my pocket and came out with a handful of coins.

"Will this help?"

The alien mechanics made strange, metallic hooting sounds.

"I guess that means no," I said.

One of the aliens plucked a coin out of the air and ate it.

William was looking worried.

"Listen," said Sean calmly, "everyone just relax. It's not a problem."

He started taking things out of his pockets: felt-tipped pens, erasers, licorice all-sorts and chocolates, wind-up toys, a small radio, elastic bands, football cards, a telescope, a pocket video game. It kept coming. Sean's pockets were bottomless. The spaceship was filling up with his floating treasures.

The alien mechanics fell silent. They were intrigued, they were in awe. They'd never seen so much stuff in all their lives.

"I think," said Sean with a smile, "that we can make some kind of deal here."

It wasn't long before the mechanics were hard at work. They hooked up a new battery and fired up the spaceship's engine, and we all tumbled to the floor as the gravity came back on.

"Thank goodness for your pockets," I said to Sean.

"Thank goodness for your quick thinking," Sean said to me.

We were best friends again, I could tell.

"And now," said William, "homewards for you both!"

The Earth looked like a picture from the school atlas as we plunged down through blue sky. After a few seconds, I could see the town, then my neighbourhood, then the field behind our house, and before I knew it we were on the ground.

I jumped out of the hatch and rolled on the grass. I was so glad to be back home! Everything looked

different and new. How could I have
thought it was boring?

"William," I said, "that was a
fantastic trip! Thank you."

"You are most welcome," he said.

I hesitated, then asked, "Can I
take a picture of you before you go?"

"Very well, Ian."

He stood up in the hatchway of his spaceship.

I raised the camera to my eye, and pressed the button, but knew instantly that something was wrong.

"Hey, there's no film in my camera!"

I patted my pockets for all the other rolls I'd taken – nothing!

"All my film's gone, too!" exclaimed Sean.

"The mechanics!" I cried. "They must have swiped it when they were working on the ship!"

"They probably ate it!" said Sean. "Rotten alien mechanics!"

"Nay, it was not the mechanics," William said. "It was I."

Dangling from his fingers was all the film we'd shot off in the spaceship.

"But what about the contest?" Sean shouted.

"I thought you wanted us to take photographs!" I said in confusion.

"I wanted you to behold the wonders of the cosmos, sure enough," William replied. "But there are some things, good sirs, that must be kept secret for now. And verily, who would believe these cosmic snapshots of yours?" He bowed with a grand flourish, and twinkled his eyes at me. "Yet rest assured, I give you my best, for victory in your earthly photo contest! Until next time!"

The hatch clanged shut, and the spaceship streaked up into the sky in a bolt of blue lightning.

"What a rip off," muttered Sean, kicking at stones as we walked home. "We'll never win first prize now. An exploding planet! Now *that* was a picture!"

"Cheer up," I said, looking around happily. "We've got a whole planet of our own to take pictures of."

The MERMAID at No.13

Gyles Brandreth

What *do* you do when you find a mermaid sitting in the bath?

If you're Hamlet Brown you take a good look, swallow hard, turn round and run out of the room as fast as you can.

The trouble is that no one will believe him, least of all his goodie-goodie sister, Susan. But there *is* a mermaid in the bath, Hamlet knows it, and he sets about proving it.

MR MAJEIKA
and the
Haunted Hotel

Humphrey Carpenter

Spooks and spectres at the *Green Banana*!

Class Three of St Barty's are off on an outing to Hadrian's Wall with their teacher, Mr Majeika (who happens to be a magician). Stranded in the fog when the tyres of their coach are mysteriously punctured, they take refuge in a nearby hotel called the Green Banana. Soon some very spooky things start to happen. Strange lights, ghostly sounds and vanishing people...